WHO IS THOMAS LIGOTTI?

ALBERTO D. HETMAN

Edited by Jude Keast

Copyright © 2021 by Alberto D. Hetman

ALL RIGHTS RESERVED. NO PART OF THIS PUBLICATION MAY BE REPRODUCED, STORED IN A RETRIEVAL SYSTEM, DISTRIBUTED OR TRANSMITTED, IN ANY FORM OR BY ANY MEANS, ELECTRONIC, MECHANICAL, PHOTOCOPYING, RECORDING, OR OTHERWISE WITHOUT THE PRIOR WRITTEN PERMISSION OF THE COPYRIGHT OWNER. THE SCANNING, UPLOADING AND DISTRIBUTION OF THIS BOOK VIA THE INTERNET, OR VIA ANY OTHER MEANS, WITHOUT THE PERMISSION OF THE AUTHOR, IS ILLEGAL AND PUNISHABLE BY LAW. PLEASE PURCHASE ONLY AUTHORIZED ELECTRONIC EDITIONS, AND DO NOT PARTICIPATE IN OR ENCOURAGE ELECTRONIC PIRACY OF COPYRIGHTED MATERIALS. YOUR SUPPORT OF THE AUTHORS' RIGHTS IS APPRECIATED.

FIRST EDITION 2021

This book is a work of fiction. These stories and characters are fictitious. The author might or might not share the views expressed by the imaginary or real persons mentioned throughout this work. Certain real names are mentioned as reference only. The author did not intend to offend them in any way. For other names, any resemblance to real people, living or dead, is purely coincidental. Some places described in this work are entirely imaginary. Certain long-standing institutions, such as newspapers, are mentioned with deepest respect.

ISBN 9798522131746

Design by Alberto D. Hetman

To *Andrew* and *Julian*

aut viam inveniam aut faciam

CONTENTS

Acknowledgments	i
A Macabre Incident	1
120 Years	7
The Religion of the Atheists	15
Who is Thomas Ligotti?	23
Batman (of Summerhill)	29
Brother Seymour	37
Chess Games	47
The Dead	53
Ouroboros	63
16 Years	73
Pebble in a Sandbox	83
It is thus Proved	91

ACKNOWLEDGMENTS

I owe my greatest debt of gratitude to my wife, Silvina, for reading all my stories before they were edited. For listening to me, always.

I would like to thank Jude Keast for editing this book, all his help and advice. Without his help this book would not be possible.

Arturo de Witte, thank you for being a friend I trust and respect. I will always be grateful to you for writing a synopsis for my book.

A very special thanks to Helen Nelson. You were right!

A MACABRE INCIDENT

I needed to earn my daily bread. I was hired as a watchman by St. James' Cemetery. The pay was not bad but it was not one of those jobs of which you made a career. It was a night shift job. I took it for granted that during the first weeks my eyes would close by themselves. I would start at six in the evening, just after the gates closed, working until six the next morning – six days a week, Tuesday until Sunday. I was told I would start January 2nd. I accepted – there was not much of a choice.

I was told to be an hour early on the first day for a training session. It was simple: I would work the shift with another watchman, a retired policeman, in alternating two hour parts. I would carry a gun even though I did not know how to use it. The man who hired me was in his fifties and this job was his livelihood. He jokingly said that I should not be afraid of ghosts, "...the dead are dead. Here we have only bones."

"Occasionally," he said, "we catch a parapsychologist who jumps the fence at night to conduct who knows what kind of experiment. We have also had a couple of cases where plaques have been stolen. Despite repeated warnings, family members still place bronze plaques on the marble. That is tempting fate – but they do not understand. How can we guard every tomb with only two watchmen? Do you know how many tombs there are? And, of course, there are watchmen who claim to have heard everything from voices to crying – well, I will spare you. If you ask me, I have never heard or seen anything like that. We should not be afraid of the dead but of the living. Everything else is a lie."

He gave me the gun and explained the schedule. I started the first part of the shift, from 6 to 8 P.M. I had a job.

***

The first part of the shift ended. So as not to scare me, the other watchman came up in front of me and told me it was already five minutes after 8. Coffee was brewing in the office. He seemed a sullen fellow – more dead than alive.

I took advantage of my two free hours to call home and speak to my wife. I drank two cups of coffee and amused myself by watching a cat turning on itself, clawing at the air. If every night was going to be as quiet as this one, I said to myself, then I had to bring a book to read so as not to get bored.

The second part of my shift was from 10 until

midnight. There were no incidents to report.

The third part of my shift, and the last one in my case, started at 2 A.M. I lingered a while, spying some dates on the tombstone of a woman who had died at the age of 22. Suddenly raindrops fell on my head and, having no umbrella, I quickened my pace. But it did not rain; those first few drops were all the rain we had that night.

About 100 feet from me I could see the light of flashlights. To give myself confidence, I caressed the butt of the gun. I walked silently, crouching behind the tombstones. I lay face down and, sticking my head out from the edge of a tombstone, saw three men in front of an open coffin. A flashlight was on the mound illuminating an open grave and another one was on the coffin lid illuminating the three men.

Two of them, shovels in hand, wore jeans and sweaters. They were average looking men. The third one, his hand caressing the coffin, wore a dark suit, white shirt and a dark tie.

One of the two men said, "Hurry up! We do not have all night. Someone will see us."

The other one, first rubbing his forehead, took a black garbage bag and, taking the bones out of the coffin, put them in the bag.

The man in the suit, by prying the lid of the coffin, opened it completely and got inside. From his suit he pulled out a wallet, counted some bills and, dividing them equally, gave them to the two men. The sum had apparently been agreed on beforehand, as they voiced no complaint. Then he leaned back into the coffin without saying a word.

The two men closed the coffin and lowered it into

the grave with the aid of ropes. It was surely done this way to avoid hurting the man wearing the suit. Then they started shovelling. It took them eight minutes to fill up the grave from the mound. Not even for a second did they stop their work. Not a word was exchanged, not even to ask themselves why they were doing this. Perhaps they already knew?

In all that time I kept thinking – I should do something. I was paid to be a watchman. But it was also true that this my first day at work and I was not going to risk my life for three madmen. So here I was, lying on a grave, watching two men burying a man wearing a suit.

At the end, one of the men said to the other: "That didn't take long. The bones...do you get rid of them or do I?" referring to the bones in the garbage bag, the last vestige of the real owner of the tomb. I did not hear the answer. They turned off the flashlights and left. I saw them jumping the fence and would never see them again in my life.

I kept thinking this was a New Year's joke. Was it not January 2nd after all?

I waited half an hour but no one came back. In the next half hour I investigated the tomb. In a hurry, some fragments of marble had being placed on it at random. Apparently they had broken the marble while digging up the grave. They did not touch the bronze plaque with the inscription noting the date of death – 18 years ago. An empty vase was lying on the side. I picked it up with my hands, placing it back where it should be. I did not hear a voice coming from the grave. Placing my hand on the grass, I did not notice any shaking. If the man wanted it so, he was dead.

The third shift ended but I kept thinking about this macabre incident. Should I have made an attempt to stop these men? If I said something now would I not lose my job? My conscience told me that this was wrong. But it was now too late to do anything about it.

The retired policeman returned at almost 6. Nothing of note had occurred he said, "…like every other night."

***

The next day there was nothing in the newspapers about this incident. I went to the cemetery to see the grave (which had being paid up for thirty years) and found it as I had left it the night before. I found a half-smoked cigarette thrown aside. Although the marble was broken, this may have happened before the incident as many years had passed. The inscription was undamaged – not even a scratch on it.

With the exception of that day I never returned to the grave. In my patrols, I avoided it. Did anyone leave flowers in the vase? Was it ever visited by family members? I do not know. At least no one complained about the condition of the marble.

For the next three months there were no other incidents to report. Then I quit. I could not get used to the midnight shift.

I have not stopped asking myself – why? And who was that third man? I do not know.

Who is Thomas Ligotti?

120 YEARS

As everyone knows, walking is good for the muscles. And also exercising the lungs daily – taking a deep breath, filling them up with air and then emptying them completely. Doing so can rejuvenate you, taking off the years so as not to look as wrinkled as an old scroll from the Pentateuch. Or so say those who have a belief in such prescriptions for all ills.

If it is hot, the sun hits you in the head (not literally, of course!) and you become a victim of sunstroke; if it is cold your nose drips like a faucet that is not completely turned off. That is why the "Indian Summer" of North America is the most favorable time of year for a walk around Toronto. There is neither a danger of burning nor freezing.

As I sat on a bench in front of St. Michael's Cathedral it came to me how badly people in the so-called first world countries eat. That is why a 36 year old friend of mine, Steve, has already has had a cardiac arrest. And Susana, another friend, needs to balance her diet – eating this, not eating that – so her cholesterol does not kill her. Life is curious, because despite these examples, people in Canada live long lives. It is also true, as most immigrants to this country say, that there are very few children seen on the streets.

Interrupting these circumstantial digressions, and on a whim, I suddenly decided to eat a chocolate bar I kept in a pocket. After filling my mouth with its half sweet taste, I continued reading a book by Lord Dunsany which I had been greedily observing on a shelf in my library.

For a moment I forgot that I was sitting there reading and meditating, not looking up from the page of the book open on my lap. I did not realize that someone was sitting next to me when suddenly an old man leaned his cane against the back of the bench and cleared his throat. He looked at me as a shipwrecked sailor at the mercy of salt water would, when spying a faraway boat through his rusty telescope. "You like reading? Me too. It is one of those evils that I carry from when I was a teenager. It has become an obsession, and, over the years, it has taken so much of my time that the 24-hour day seems shorter than it really is." (In Toronto, to tell the truth, old people often talk to passersby without caring whether they are being paid attention to or not. They are alone and strangers provide the only relief they have left to them.)

I replied that I like to read, but not much (lying about it), that the real reason was to be at this corner enjoying the fresh air "…try it yourself. Sit here for half an hour and you will start to feel healthy." The man was older than Methuselah, and that is why I talked to him. I tend not to go away leaving them with half said words in their mouths.

He showed me a book. "This is my favorite book, *Anthology of Latin American Short Stories*." Then, looking at me more closely as would a watchmaker looking at some scattered gears on a table, he asked: "Where do you come from?" I thought my foreign accent was no longer noticeable, and raising my eyebrows, ignored his question. What would come next: a request for coins or a coffee or cigarettes?

"Homo Dei by Beinaravicius. Have you read it?" he said. As he had done, I looked at his face trying to find a clue as to what country he was from. The accent was Portuguese, perhaps from the Azores Islands. Those I had met so far were superstitious, worked like horses and were uncomfortable when I told them I read – as exactly as Saramago described them in his books.

"Yes, I have read it," I confessed. "Why?" He smiled as if he had achieved his goal in life, and then he read me the following paragraph:

"Why do good and honest people have the same fate, or worse, than murderers, the corrupt, etc. Both, at the end of life, end up in the same place."

He seemed to be excited, reading hastily. He turned a page and his finger went down until he found what he wanted, his hand smoothing the page as he continued:

"So I said: How good it would be, if the life of a good person at heart, doing good work because he felt it in his soul, would be increased five minutes or even 30 seconds for every good and

honorable gesture he made. For example, helping a little girl who is alone cross the street, giving alms, helping the elderly – but not as a job or a duty. If we had in this society such an honest person living an unspecified additional time, would we not have something like the good God that the gospel tells us about?"

"Do you believe it is possible," he said

I replied that I did not. "One dies when the circumstances determine it so," I said. He sat back, closing the book and taking the cane in his hand. I thought he was about to leave as mysteriously as he had appeared. "People believe whatever they want," I added so as not to annoy him. I feared he would take out a knife and try to stab me. But what could he do to me, as he looked to be more than 100 years old. I did not even understand how he could keep sitting on the bench talking to me, as if he had all the time in the world.

"I just turned 120, I want some more." He stretched out his arms to show me that he kept himself in shape. (As I said before, it is not unusual for people here to live a long life.) Just then a couple from some Slavic country interrupted us. They turned to me wondering if they were far from Parliament Street. I told them to continue going straight, "…keep going, about four more blocks; you cannot get lost because there is an antique shop in the corner." I then leaned back on the bench as one would as if setting foot on land again.

The old man waited for me to refute what he had so eagerly read. "What Beinaravicius wrote is a short story. Do you understand?" I said. I thought about it for a while as he expected an answer. My habit is to meditate on what I read, to look at it from every angle, but this time it was not easy. What would happen, I thought, if people did good deeds solely to earn extra minutes of life. For example, by saving a girl from being hit by a car I would gain an extra five minutes of life. If I were to save others – 10 or 15 more minutes. What if I were to give alms to those lying in the street having only the clothes they were wearing? Would the only question I ask be: how many minutes would God give me for my alms – 2 minutes for 10 dollars? And for helping the elderly as I was doing with this old man? I could not believe that God would reward me for such a righteous action. People commit good or bad actions according to their nature, not for receiving rewards granted by the Almighty. This was the key and so I let him know what I thought.

"Imagine a man who knows that helping others and doing good in general gives him extra minutes of life. Would we not then have a person who does good, not for its own sake, but only to win those extra minutes? Does anyone believe that in such a large universe God insists on following the acts of each one of us? But then, perhaps, adding minutes is an automatic process like sweating or healing. Hmm, don't you think so?" I turned up the collar of my coat because a cold wind was blowing in from the lake. In a few minutes we should go.

He lifted his cane then hit the asphalt on the sidewalk with it several times, without any sign of being fatigued by the effort. "I told you, 120 years. I always do good. Yes, I rather think it is automatic, that the minutes just add up in one's life. How do you believe that God would allow me to live, if he knew that what I did was out of selfishness, just to earn more minutes for my life? I have seen my grandchildren dying, and I am still alive." He coughed a little. And I noticed that forcing him to talk caused him to lose command of his English vocabulary, while infusing his speech with words of the dialect of the Azores Islands. "For 70 years I do good, ever since I read this book for the first time." He hit the cane forcefully against his leg. "Not the same book, I have thrown it away several times, and as many times, have bought it again. Homo Dei, I have read it again and again over the years, so that I think I know every sentence by heart in the same way as some know the Bible."

Squirrels were nibbling who knows what on one side of the bench, and when I turned my eyes back to the old man, I saw him leaving aided by his cane. The sun was setting in the direction he was taking. He was rushing – because he had a short time to live? Or because some dissatisfaction was gnawing at his soul? Will there be pure souls who do good without reward, or are we as Satan described us in the book of Job? The sunset was beautiful, like so many others. And like on so many evenings I got up for a walk, to go to a couple of bookstores and add to my library a different book which would sit a long time before it was read.

I looked down to check that I was not leaving anything on the bench and saw the old man had left his book. I thought of running after him to give it back but I let him go without worrying him. He would probably say it was done on purpose to earn points, thereby prolonging his life a few more minutes. Surely he had left the book on the bench because he knew I envied him, looking at him in the same way as a murderer does who is fascinated by his victim. It was an old book, maybe 50 years old – how much would it be worth? I shook my head and said I would not sell it unless I were in need again.

I took the book, putting it side by side with that of Lord Dunsany's, and headed for the subway. Within minutes I would know which bookstore to go to. There was not much to think about as there were a couple which always had the same books and thus I discarded them.

What would it matter to me if my life ended this afternoon? I have never wanted to be rewarded for being who I am.

Who is Thomas Ligotti?

THE RELIGION
OF THE ATHEISTS

As the afternoon went by, I kept thinking that today you can start your own religion simply by doing it. Look around – there are always followers willing to believe anything.

One that was in vogue (whether or not it was a true religion) was called by some "the religion of the atheists". It was also known as "the scientific religion" and "the scientific faith". It began with one temple opening its doors and a year later two more. But after five years there was only one again and that first one closed its doors for good a couple of years later. These days the building has been abandoned: there are some who claim it will be a tear down, while others say it will be turned into condos, taking advantage of its location near Lake Ontario. Walk down Dufferin Street to King Street, then keeping walking south. Ask a pedestrian, particularly if he is older and therefore know more, and he will tell you with enviable accuracy where you can find the temple of the religion of the atheists. The sign at the entrance remains, and although the paint is fading, damaged by the winter snows and the heat of the afternoon summer sun, it can still be read:

TEM_ _ _
O_
THE SCIENT_ _ _ _   _ _ _ IGION

While the paint is peeling off, and more will not be there next summer, it does not prevent you from reading most of the letters and guessing at the missing ones. Underneath the third sentence (THE SCIENT_ _ _ _   _ _ _ IGION) the Star of David is seen with the following multiplication written in its center:

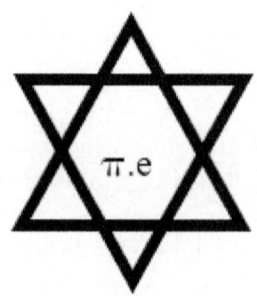

I assume that everyone knows the number Pi (π), while "e", although less known, is Euler's number. The multiplication of the two gives the approximate result of 8.53. No one has been able to explain to me whether this number has any religious or scientific meaning. Perhaps it was chosen at random. Both religion and science are silent before this mystery.

In the practice and appearance of the religion of the atheists you could find: from Tibetan Buddhism, that lunatic preference for brightly colored clothes and crew cuts; from Catholicism, the placing of small statues in niches on the side walls and on the altar a display of a woman with a small child in her arms; from other Christian religions, a preference for Russian Orthodox icons and the assiduous reading of the book by Mary Baker Eddy of Christian Science (although I swear they gave a different meaning to the original words). They also included rites from Islam and other religions and other rites based on science that were, I believe, made a posteriori, such as "The Gauss Prayer" or "The Newton Mass". Its ecumenism tried to encompass all faiths in one and then merge them with the principles of science.

In their ceremonies on a typical Sunday morning you could find a reading of the Bible, the Book of Mormon, the Bhagavad Gita, or an explanation of the origin of the universe based on the Big Bang theory. This attempt to merge religion and science initially attracted members of other religions. Wasn't it after all the first attempt to merge science and religion? It is even said that Schwalbeg[1] joined this faith for a few years. They displayed the cross, baptized their members, accepted circumcision and respected the

---

[1] Atheist philosopher and writer, author of the bestseller, "Man without God". His extensive bibliography highlights among others the book "Being an Atheist in Modern Times", which the Pope himself condemned, asserting that its reading was harmful for healthy youths and responsible adults attempting to follow a moral pathway.

Ramadan. In their printed almanac each day the birthday of a famous scientist was noted but December 25 was of course reserved for Christ. Not to do so would have been anathema. Who could be against a religion whose followers defended the beliefs of all religions and also adopted the most serious postulates of science and preached them in their temples? Who among us?

As to a religious hierarchy, they did not adopt one in particular so as not to antagonize other religions. In their temple you could find a bit of everything. It was said that all a man needed, along with a faith to believe in something greater than himself, was a hierarchy which you ascended over the years based on merit. Your opinion was taken into account. With some traditional religions man is treated as spoiled or as a number or thing, in which those at the bottom are always "at the bottom".

While there was a priest for the Christian Catholic followers, the Jewish members called him Rabbi, while others addressed him as pastor, father or bishop. For some reason, still unknown to me, they dressed in the style of the Hare-Krishna although this was not required of those occasional visitors who on one or another day might come to the temple.

(At this point I must digress to note that the scientific religion also included the faiths of the Chaldeans, Egyptians, Babylonians and other ancient civilizations. They called out to God, Pan, Zeus or Baal. For this bizarre practice they were called pagans. But keeping their heads high they made us see that there was nothing wrong in being called a pagan or living a licentious life as depicted by the three fauns in the painting "Mars and Venus" by Botticelli.)

As a sacred text they adopted the book "A Brief History of Time" by Stephen Hawking, adding fragments from the Bible, the Gita and the Koran. In the appendix there was the proof that the square root of two is an irrational number, Euclid's five postulates, Kepler's three laws and the laws of Torricelli and Boyle-Mariot among others. Some members went further and added whole passages from the Book of Mormon, the book of Christian Science, the Egyptian Book of the Dead and the Popul Vuh of the Maya. Other followers added "Cosmos" by Carl Sagan and the short story "The Three Versions of Judas" by Jorge Luis Borges. They rejected the tithe. They asserted that tomorrow will bring its own worries. Those of other faiths who were captivated by the new religion nodded in agreement while affirming that God protects both us and the birds.

From comments that came to my ears, what most caught the attention of both experts and laymen were the putting together of those two contradictory words: "religion" on the one side, "atheist" on the other. Can there be a religion without God? But what is important about religion are its rituals, the adherence to tradition and the getting together with others – not the existence of God.

With the sentences "based on..." or "adapted from..." you would find mainly Christian songs in the hymnal. But, as new followers joined, the melodies of Buddhist chants were added along with songs from contemporary rock 'n roll musicians such as "ob-la-di, ob-la-da" by the Beatles or the song "I am happy because I am" that always preceded the Newton Mass.

They sang in a euphoric way, but not shouting and not muttering; there was clearly a passion in the voices of the followers of this religion. Instead of the classical piano or organ, the melodies were played with a glockenspiel. The accompaniment was done with a Turkish ud, the sistrum and the tambourine. It was forbidden to call out "hurray" or "bravissimo" or to applaud. I was not told why, but I suspect that it was out of respect for ancient religious traditions forbidding them.

They explained the errors of religion scientifically. They believed that St. Thomas Aquinas' need for an "unmoved mover" of the universe was wrong. Instead they taught the Big Bang theory without the need for God. Darwin's theory of evolution was also taught. A number of times I came across sermons which invited listeners to wonder about mysteries that had worried the uneducated for three or four millennia. Questions such as: Why did God create dinosaurs only to have them eliminated overnight? To turn them into oil as many wrongly believe? Or why did he create giraffes with such long necks? Is it not better to examine these questions by applying the theory of evolution? Thinking was fundamental. It was about answering questions without relying on the traditional approach of invoking the action of God and his plans. I was told that the most famous atheists have been those who have asked themselves: "Why are we here?" "Who are we?" "Where do we come from and where are we going?" Hence, the observation of the universe through a telescope was mandatory.

They recommended the assiduous reading of the Book of Job because it spoke of a God who cared little about humanity. They even dared to replace it with a "revised version of the Book of Job". It emphasized the brutal way in which God killed Job's family and pointed out that it would have been simpler to drive his family into exile.

They believed in the resurrection of Christ, but also in re-incarnation. To support this view they based their belief on the real-life cases that were reported in Moody's bestseller, "Life after Life". These cases were accepted as true to the point that followers would have killed anyone who claimed that they were lies. And why not? Do not members of traditional religions kill those who attempt to demonstrate the falsity of their beliefs?

Their meetings, following in the Christian tradition, were on Wednesday nights (for young people), Saturdays and Sundays. In the morning there was "Sunday School" where children were taught that God did not exist and that logic should always prevail over faith. In their Sunday sermons they would talk about Buddha, then Christ and finally St. Francis of Assisi. An hour later they would refute the existence of God. How was this possible? In answer they quoted Khalil Gibran: "No Faith stood after the Prophet Muhammad and Christ to shed its light"[2]. They believed that Zoroaster, Buddha, Jesus and Muhammad, as well as others, were great men and for that reason should be read regularly. Unlike in other religions where they are read to kill time.

A few wanted to separate from the religion of the atheists and found another religion where you could

---

[2] From the book "The Procession" by Khalil Gibran, 1958.

believe in both the existence and non-existence of God. Were they not seen as lunatics? I would have to say so, although if someone believes there is no logic to it, it is because they did not attend the hour of worship where it was explained. If the probability that God exists, as to the probability that he does not is 50 – 50, then both propositions must be true. According to this logic, therefore, the existence of God is refuted for those who do not believe and proved for those who do. The advocates of this theory argued that with practice you could accept this approach as natural and logical. There was no schism over this question, however. On the contrary, we remained united until the end.

At one point we had over five thousand followers. But after seven years we were forced to close our doors forever as there were only twelve still attending every single day of worship (the same number as the apostles of Christ). At our last meeting we auctioned off the last few belongings that had not been sold to pay that month's rent. We remembered, swept away by a sickly nostalgia, the good old days when the newspapers talked about us and our songs were played over the radio. By good fortune I won the glockenspiel, the hymnals and a statue of a fat Buddha.

When the sign of the scientific religion is brought down, nobody will talk about us ever again.

WHO IS THOMAS LIGOTTI?

I rubbed my eyes vigorously with both hands and decided to read what I had written without stopping until the final period of the last sentence. It could have any one of these final titles, I said to myself, such as:
"Who is Thomas Ligotti?"
"The Conspiracy of Thomas Ligotti"
Or simply:
"The Non-Existence of Thomas Ligotti"
The first time, I read what I had written in an exaggeratedly loud voice, such as you would read to a person who was going deaf (not one who was born deaf, to whom it would have been useless to even speak). Then I read it in silence, scanning it with my eyes, in the same way as those who read their Bibles in church:
"Thomas Ligotti does not exist. This writer of ominous short stories and essays of horror is merely the invention of other writers, some of the stature of

Ramsey Campbell or Clive Barker."

Of these two I was sure: of others, I could name some names but could not swear that these choices would be right. This theory was not original. It had been proposed unsuccessfully by Gwilym Games a few years ago.

There was little evidence that Thomas Ligotti existed. Only a few short stories signed by him, the signatures almost identical and some scarce photographs of which only three were known. Unlike Gwilym Games, my approach focused on what others have said, taking each of their assertions, then refuting them one by one logically and noting the contradictions between them. Probably I wanted to believe that this was a case like that of Martin Margiela, a prestigious Belgian designer, of whom there is no known photograph of as an adult. Although he continues to exhibit his new clothing collections and his brand has acquired a reputation over the years, he appears neither in his fashion shows, nor in the group photos, where his place is marked by an empty chair. So does Margiela exist? Does Ligotti exist?

The three known photographs of him are (I dare to say) identical – taken in the same minute but from different angles. He was born in 1953 in Detroit, yet it seems strange that nobody has shown up with some old school photograph or one of him standing next to a childhood friend. Nor has anyone come forward offering to sell a photograph of him, proving once and for all that Ligotti exists. But this has not been the case.

Ligotti seems only to have but an invented past, one as improbable as some of his most famous stories... That he received two Bram Stoker awards in 1996. Yes, but what does that prove? Where are the photographs and the testimonials of those who saw him receiving the awards? The biography of Ligotti seems to have borrowed some fragments of that of Nathaniel Hawthorne's, whom it is said, spent two years living as a recluse. Which is extremely curious: had Hawthorne not been a politician for several years? How then could he have lived a life inside four walls, preserved his sanity and later represented his country? ...Does that make any sense whatsoever?

Some literary critics point out that Ligotti was in and out of psychiatric institutions... Ligotti: a madman? But is that not a contradiction for it is also said that he worked for a firm in Detroit for 23 straight years. Here we seem to have some of the influence of Jean Ray, who invented his own autobiography claiming to have travelled all over the world as a sailor on a ship (What ship? When?); to have been an arms trafficker (would an arms trafficker shout such news about himself from the rooftops?) and other lies that had me laughing to myself.

The rest of my essay consisted of data: dates, names, addresses all of which could be verified and which confirmed that Ligotti had no existence before the 1980's. It was if he was born all of a sudden, like the Golem of Meyrink. I give him the same real existence as that of the character in "The Circular Ruins" by Borges who no one saw disembarking in the unanimous night. I had wanted to include Borges among the creators of Ligotti but he was already dead at that time.

I received a letter from Mark Samuels, author of

"Vrolyck" and the "The Metempsychosis of William Brooks" among other stories. He said he had been offered a sum of money (without specifying how much) to add something to the Gestalt personality of Ligotti. This is my final proof but you will have to trust me on this point as I have lost the letter.

Finally, although I prefer not to let you know the reasons, I see in the personality of Ligotti, the stroke of the pens of Ramsey Campbell, Clive Barker and others. As I have said, they flatly deny this fact.

But what of the interviews with Ligotti? ...What of them? Many interviews are works of fiction, having never happened. Many, and I would not be wrong in saying this with a certainty, almost all, are written a posteriori, the writer sitting in front of a computer, pondering each word, copying quotations, inflating phrases like birthday balloons with air.

I should finish here, I said, with my conclusion that Thomas Ligotti, so vast, so exquisite with words, so sunken in the mantle of deepest mystery, does not exist.

***

The sun must be setting because the evening light began to fade very quickly. "What do you think about what I have read to you?" I asked Thomas Ligotti, who sat in front of me, leaning to one side against a window in his house in Florida.

He did not answer. I had imagined that he would say that, some time ago, somewhere, he had heard that theory. But he did not say it. He said nothing. I wanted him to tell me that he realized that what I had written would only make his existence more unreal than it was already.

While he sat there facing me, I could see no resemblance in him to any of the three photographs that I had already viewed. I did not see him as a Rasputin (whose likeness, as he said to me, was that which they thought he would have looked like a long time ago). When I saw him sideways in the still blinding light of the setting sun, I thought I was seeing the face of Hodgson (William Hope Hodgson) or was I wrong, perhaps it was that of Mark Twain. When he turned back to me a few fragments from Hesse's Siddhartha came to mind and I saw in him the face of all mortals: that of a beggar, that of a rich man, that of an adulterer, that of an ordinary man walking down a dusty road in some remote and unheard of place. If I had taken a photograph of him at that moment, would everyone who viewed it see him as such? Then I thought I could see through him, as if he were invisible, leaving only a silhouette -- the invention of the imagination of other writers.

I preferred, however, to tell him simply that he looked like the astronaut Scranton, the man in the story by Ballard, who had walked on the moon.

He went back to looking out the window and just said to me: "Scranton, eh?" Then he roared with laughter. If someone had whispered in the ear of H.P. Lovecraft that many people said he did not exist either, would he have laughed the same way? These are questions for which we will never know the answers.

Who is Thomas Ligotti?

BATMAN
(OF SUMMERHILL)

He began to be seen around Yonge Street and St. Clair Avenue with an almost religious regularity. This Batman, whom some incorrectly called the Batman of Summerhill (incorrectly, because Summerhill subway station is 7 blocks to the south), appeared suddenly out of nowhere like a rabbit from a magician's hat. Within weeks people got used to the mask, the original Batman mask from the 1966 TV series. Also, the distrust with which he was greeted in the first days totally disappeared in the following month. He did not beg and bothered no one. Anyone would swear that his appearance at the corner must be some kind of joke. At first some looked all around to see if there was some hidden camera sticking out of a window or a van. What other logical and rational explanation could there be? In order to stand out from the crowd, I discarded conventional explanations and proposed to people that Batman was only a student at the University of Toronto who was studying the behaviour of people facing an unheard of situation. But Batman took no notes, a simple observation that shattered my theory.

If you dare to look around at this corner of Yonge and St. Clair, viewing your fellowmen, you would see two guys begging, each in their own way.

The first one is a street artist, a guitarist of about 50. The electric guitar is connected to a small speaker at his feet. He plays old variations by Dowland or more modern ones by the Beatles. Sometimes I have heard him playing some piece by J. S. Bach, I cannot remember which one, or fragments, I think, by Sarasate or Albéniz. However, who knows, I may be mistaken in my judgment. Passing by his side, I saw just a few dollar coins and quarters scattered in his open guitar case. He dressed in a black suit, never otherwise. And his repertoire never varied, his interpretations being repeated over the days, weeks, months. He was consistently there on the weekends, standing on the northeast corner. His guitar can be heard from afar, almost half a block away, and our ears can hear, over the honking of the taxis and trucks, those well remembered chords of Paul McCartney's Yesterday.

The second one, a short guy, no more than five feet tall, never stops begging, jumping on one leg, then the other, alternating between the two, and stretching out his hand holding a Santa Claus hat. Once, while passing by, I heard someone talking to him, advising the short guy to get a job and recommending that he go to a certain address. After this, and probably for that reason, I did not see him around for several weeks. He begged, standing in the middle of the sidewalk, or suddenly he would appear out of nowhere approaching one from the side. If only he would do a pirouette, perhaps even the most hard-hearted might give him something from time to time.

From what I have seen, people considered them so much a part of the landscape, that they would not even steal a glance at them, no more than they would at the two churches one block to the north.

And that's all, omitting the geography of the place with its bars, expensive buildings, embassies and banks at its four corners.

Batman was no match for these two. Simply because he did not beg, a fact that, on the one hand horrified the many, and on the other made them think: So what does he want? Many times I have compared this Batman to the one in the old Batman TV episodes and, although I have seen the TV series, I have unfortunately been unable to draw any conclusions about him from this.

Batman's routine was as precise as a clock. On weekdays, in the evening between 6:15 and 7:30, Batman was on the northwest corner, in front of the building that housed the radio station and newsstand store. He stood as RANTES in the film "Man Facing Southeast" by Subiela, precisely facing southeast looking …at the bank of Montreal? …at the revolving doors on the corner? …at the birds being fed by lonely souls? …at what? Then, between 7:30 and 8:00, he crossed to the southwest corner and looked at the northeast. And finally, between 8:00 and 8:30 approximately, since I have never seen him looking at a watch on his wrist, he lay like a dog next to the wall on the northeast corner. He lay face up, as if he were sleeping or was squinting at distant stars in the night sky.

On weekends he appeared briefly for twenty minutes to meet his viewers. He limited himself to crossing the street, one side to the other, east to west, north to south, and vice versa, completing an imaginary square. People, who had at first avoided him out of fear of a man wearing a mask, now passed by him as if they were best of friends although those who had never seen him laughed or shouted at him: "you are fucking crazy".

His mask was worn out. It had come apart over the months revealing parts of his face. I think that this bothered people more than seeing him there every day. A worn out mask showed untidiness, dirt, neglect, nihilism. The police never held him for questioning because he had never committed any crime such as the petty crime of watching a neighbor's wife which is so common these days. He appeared, after all, to be a nice guy. I should add that his clothes were not Batman's. He was dressed fashionably. His clothes could have been bought at the Salvation Army building a few blocks past St. Clair and Bathurst Street which he probably did so as not give any clue that would reveal who he was.

Only once did I see him talking to someone else. About what, I do not know, but the conversation lasted for nearly half an hour.

For months nothing changed, his routine remained the same, repeated week after week to the point of boredom. As the months passed the guy stopped being interesting to me. I kept wondering, with the coming of winter, whether we would still see him standing there. That routine, as certain and unchangeable as the ingratitude of human beings today, ended in late September, near the end of autumn. It was not a cold day, nor was it a windy afternoon, nor would the evening be as rainy as it had been a few days ago.

That afternoon Batman seemed to be dying, twisted in pain lying on one side on the sidewalk. People passed by him paying no attention, as if they were used to the most unprecedented of events: death, the pain of others. As if it were normal to see Batman lying there. I came near to him, not out of compassion or curiosity, or to fulfill a debt to my conscience (if I have one). I do not know why, but I knelt beside him, and without saying anything or asking permission, rubbed my hands gently on his shoulder, his back, his forearm. His eyes were light blue, clear like my mother's on her deathbed, a few days before she died. They could have been the eyes of either a young or old man. What could one see behind the mask? They were limpid and pure eyes of the sort that one finds at random and very rarely in one's life. And only if one has lived a long life. His teeth were white, pristine, bleached like those of the rich or of Hollywood stars.

A thick blood gushed from his slightly parted lips. I asked if he needed anything, and without saying more, I stood up looking for a public telephone to call 911. He grabbed my leg, guessing at my intention and, by moving his head from side to side a few times, made me give up seeking medical help. He stood up leaning on me. He pushed me gently, forcing me to accompany him to what proved to be his home on

Alvin Avenue half a block from St. Clair. We climbed the steps with difficulty. I said it was best to call 911. He was dying. He found his key and, upon opening the door, fell on the carpet in the middle of a room lit only by the fugitive light of an evening going slowly dark.

I could barely close the door. I called out, not knowing whether he was alone or married and that someone might be at home. I said, with Batman lying dead on the floor, that I would call 911. The house was deserted. Batman was dead. That I could swear. I went through his clothes, trying to find something that would unveil the mystery of this man. I found a diary that he kept and, as soon as I read it, put it into one of my pockets. Then I sat down to wait for help, which soon arrived and confirmed my suspicion that Batman was dead.

In the following days I met his wife and three daughters, one of whom was called Montana. They thanked me for my help. I could not tell whether their sincerity was real or feigned; whether they wept for love of this man or because they were mourning for the dead out of habit. The wife showed me pictures of Batman without his mask. They were natives of northern Ontario and had come to Toronto ten or twelve years ago. They had no money problems, no debts from gambling. She told me that Batman did not drink or smoke, that his conduct was irreproachable. This was attested to by the law firm where he went to work every morning. His last name could be clearly read on the plate at the entrance to the building that housed their offices. Batman was one of three lawyers of a reputable law firm located in the same building in which he could be found lying in front of every evening. A man of just 55 years with the whole world still in front of him.

His diary contained essays such as "On the Properties of Light"; "On the Muscles Involved in the Act of Breathing"; some poems; sketches of trees, faces, building facades; quotations from many books, some without attribution; and dates and what he had done on them as in a typical diary. Nowhere did he mention the reasons why he did what he did. No detail of cases he worked on except for a brief mention of the sums charged.

Why was he wearing a Batman's mask? Surely to hide his face, but why? In the diary he had written the following paragraph so I preferred to keep it. I do not think anyone suspected that he had kept a diary nor do I think his wife and daughters cared. And if they cared, so what? Moreover, it was too late to explain to them that, after stealing it, I was returning it to them out of a feeling of guilt.

He had written:

[…]
I see myself dead in a coffin. I am neither young nor old, and I see myself wearing Batman's mask. I don't feel shame at dying this way. In a few years, two, three, five, my wife will marry another. My daughters will remember me as Batman, not as their father. Then I see my wife dying; my daughters age, have children, and, in turn, grow old and die. And I feel lonely because everyone who ever knew me, or remembered me, or talked about me is dead. Fifty years go by, 100, 300, and I wake up. And I am not dead. My face is a little wrinkled but I am alive. I am not a ghost but a man of flesh and blood again. Where do

I go? What do I do? I can sleep in any of the four corners of St Clair and Yonge and do not need to wear a mask. If I am asked my name, I say I do not remember it. Even though I could scream my name from the rooftops, no one remembers my existence and I feel good about that. I see that there are four directions I can choose. I dismiss the south as that ends in the lake, and the north but I do not know why. Maybe because we came from the north. I say to myself that it can be either east or west… I can go wherever I want, do whatever I want – it is not too late.

My only conclusion, and at this point in the narrative I would not want to consider any other thought, is that this man was escaping from the society in which he worked so tirelessly. Why did he choose this way and not another? He said it himself when he says the following…"I see myself wearing Batman's mask. I don't feel shame at dying this way." From this one might think that he was tired of his lifestyle, his wife, his daughters, of fighting with clients every day of his life. Or one can think whatever one wants.

The truth is, that two years after his death, no one talks about Batman anymore.

BROTHER SEYMOUR

"Many cling tooth and nail to the existence of God but no one can prove he exists. This faith, blind and irrational, is usually what pushes them to keep breathing another day."
Brother Seymour

On January 2, 2001 I read in a local newspaper those few words (in 4 lines, 5 with the headline) about the death of Seymour Jørgensen (or Brother Seymour as he preferred to be called), and a score of his followers. So few words that they could be read with just a glance. The newspaper did not provide any details of Seymour's life citing only the example of fanatics who had threatened to commit mass suicide at the beginning of the new millennium. For most this was to be January 1, 2000, while for others it was to be the beginning of 2001. Seymour evidently was one of the few who shared this second opinion.

I know little or nothing about Seymour's life and

whether or not his name is listed in any up-to-date encyclopedia of Sects and Heresies. It could be, but I doubt it. I never talked to him. I only saw him twice in my life, and that from afar. His face brought to my mind the memory of a Hollywood film actor but I do not know which one. It was said that he was from Ostersund, Sweden. His accent was that of a foreigner, like that of whose parents had brought them to a new country when they were small. But wouldn't this be one more proof that his lie was so elaborate as to deceive even those who knew better?

The best I can do will be to tell what little I know about him. The bodies of his followers all had their wrists cut. It was calculated that they died bleeding over a couple of hours.

***

Stephen Hutchinson assured me he was not lying. I decided to give him the benefit of the doubt even though his account was implausible. Why would he lie to me after all? And although this question floated in the air I did not stop telling myself that what he said, as in all similar cases, could not be verified. He gave a detailed description of the unique but isolated facts of his case.

"…and for two minutes I was dead. My heart had stopped. I was dead. Doctors were moving around me, agitated, not knowing what to do. Inside I felt a peace that could not be explained with words. I felt happy for having lived. I realized that the doctors and nurses, running from one side to the other, would not understand if I was able to tell them that everything was fine, that they should let me die. Then, as mysteriously as it had stopped, my heart resumed its normal pace."

Soon after his experience I told him that a person whose heart had stopped for a few minutes was not dead. This only occurs 5 or 6 minutes after the brain has been deprived of oxygen and all the neurons die. In this case the brain dies and all that one has being disappears. Then I recommended that he read the book written by a certain "Moody", or "Dr. Moody" – I do not remember which name exactly – about those who had near death experiences.

The next week he invited me to participate in a course of 8 classes, about an hour to an hour and a half each, which would start at the beginning of the next month. (In 8 classes as is taught even today, the variants of the Ruy Lopez opening in chess). I accepted so as not to offend or annoy him. What would I gain by mentioning, as examples, cases of famous writers such as Philip K. Dick who had the same experience of being dead for a few minutes. His account did not add anything related to the peace that Stephen had stressed of his experience.

The course taught one how to die. The method was known as "Jørgensen's method" as created by Seymour Jørgensen and it seems funny to say but it was designed to teach you to die in a good way. That is what the method promised. I agreed to go with Stephen because he kept insisting that I go with him.

The instructor introduced himself as Hans Jørgensen, Seymour's brother.

LEARNING TO DIE, BY SEYMOUR JØRGENSEN

CLASS N° 1

The first half hour of the first class was introductory. It was a history lesson. Hans Jørgensen listed for us the number of religions that had existed in the world since the time of the Phoenicians. He stressed the Egyptian belief in which, when we were dying, our souls were weighed by Osiris and the idea of the voyage of our souls.

His words were vague and confusing. We did see that in some cases death can be anticipated but that in others (heart attacks, strokes, car accidents) one died quickly. In these cases we would not be able to use what he would teach us in the following classes.

He defined the concepts of the soul, immortality and death. He quoted by heart Votaires's definition of the soul indicating that it was the correct one.

In the second part of the class we were taught to forgive everyone. We sat on folding chairs in pairs that were conveniently located around the room. Then we closed our eyes and were told to visualize those we would normally never forgive in the course of our lives.

Later each one of us hit the person next to us with a dry branch just as in the days of yore when teachers taught their students discipline. We allowed our neighbor to hit us while saying, "I forgive you." Then the palms of our hands were burned with a lit cigarette as we said, one to the other, "I forgive you." No one could die in peace unless they first forgave all of the evils that had befallen them in life.

Finally, in the last half an hour, we were left alone to forgive those who had ever harmed us in our lives. It brought to my mind my brother who I had not seen in 20 years. At first I thought I could not do it but then the words came to my mouth: "I forgive you, brother." I could not believe the words that my lips were whispering.

CLASS N° 2

We were told to rest on mattresses laying on the floor. I must confess, they were comfortable. Hans Jørgensen turned on a shortwave radio without tuning it. He told us that we should focus on the noise of the static. For me, at least, it gradually made me forget the distant sounds of car horns and the barking of stray dogs. I even found it difficult to follow the thread of what he was saying: "…must finish the dreams that we would not complete in real life". He listed some examples: a love that we wanted so much but which we could not have; returning to play with the childhood dog that had died long ago; visiting the house where we were born; choosing another profession in life. He went on listing examples but I had already chosen mine. I had always dreamt of publishing a book. While I concentrated on the sound of the static from the radio, my dream came true. My book was published. I could feel it in my hands and if I had opened it I would have found stories that would make Poe himself shake in fear.

At the approach of the hour the volume of the static from the radio began to fade until it became inaudible and we awoke from the trance we had been in. Jørgensen said that when we die our minds are able to reconcile the what cannot be of our dreams with the reality of what is. "You should be prepared as death approaches and choose well because you will have only a few seconds before you die to take one of your dreams and make it a reality. You must accept that you cannot leave this life without closing at least one door and use this as a symbol for all the other doors that otherwise would never be closed."

After the class finished, I left cheered. I would try to close as many doors as I could when I got home.

CLASS N° 3

We sat in front of a small movie theater screen on which fragments of old American films, mostly "Westerns", were projected. Initially they had a length of half a minute and were joined to others with which they had no relationship in terms of content. Then appeared fragments, five seconds in length, which appeared and disappeared before our eyes, followed by faces or landscape, fleeting images that came and went in seconds, or tenths of seconds! I could barely tell them apart. Finally meaningless images flowed across the screen: a hand, a cloud, a sunset at sea, a glass, a volcano – static images unrelated to one another.

"Concentrate, let your eyes rest freely on the images. Life will leave you within the space of two breaths." Soon I heard a voice speaking to me but the language was incomprehensible. I did not matter whether it was Aramaic, the language of Christ, or Esperanto. I did not know whether it was the voice of

Hans Jørgensen or if I was imagining that it was his voice.

Two moments of my life came to my mind and do not ask me why two and not three or half a dozen. The first memory, which I could not specify, was when I was four years old. I had lived it and now it seemed so natural to remember it so perfectly. And yet I had forgotten it over all those years. I let out a smile. The second one was from 30 years later. The memory came and went as quickly as lightning striking in the distance. It was true, as Hans Jørgensen had asserted, that life had passed within the space of two breaths.

At night, while I slept, other memories came back to me in my dreams. It was if my life was escaping into the air as steam from an uncovered pot.

CLASS N° 4

I asked Stephen about the meaning of the fourth class. "The strange smell", he said, "comes from the kitchen. A fan was turned on half an hour ago next to a tray of freshly cut watermelon slices." The smell of watermelon seemed to fill the whole universe. We were invited to observe a light bulb and to imagine that we were looking down at our body sitting on the chair. Jørgensen insisted not block out the sweet smell of the watermelon which was already stifling.

Stephen told me that dying people claim that they can feel everything around them as if their bodies had become like radar. "…become like radar", I asked? "At the instant we are leaving our bodies", he said, "It is as if we can feel everything around us. It is a farewell in which one perceives everything, every centimeter of skin, one's knees, hair, teeth, toes, fingers…"

He could not have better described what I was feeling. I even felt a gentle breeze running through my body as in a fall from long ago.

I want to say that Stephen repeated to me on several occasions that Seymour was no Priest and that he had never being. He did not belong to any faith, although he was not an atheist. He called himself Brother Seymour to differentiate himself from the others just as some call themselves Professor or Doctor without being affiliated with any college or university.

So far, in the four classes, I had not learned to die as Seymour had promised in one of his pamphlets.

CLASS N° 5

It was only left to accept one's death as a natural fact, occurring at a specific time. I had that feeling of déjà vu, knowing that I would die and when. It was so easy to understand everything. Almost at the end I realized, as I had so many times in my life, that same certain and unmistakable feeling that I could hold in my hands and make mine. I remembered a fragment of an afternoon of yesteryear as if seen through a thick fog when I had had that same feeling of knowing why I had been born.

It was the certainty of knowing the day, the hour and the minute on which I would die; and although I could not explain why, I was happy knowing that I was going to die, that finally the agony of feeling moribund among millions was going to end.

CLASS N° 6

That Jørgensen used Stephen's experience, and also that of others' gathered there to justify his idea, did not seem right. You could always find cases in which near death experiences happened differently. Stephen said: "…when my heart stopped, I had peace, but another, a new peace that I had never imagined. My life fitted together as exactly as does one jigsaw piece to another. It was as if I loved everybody equally. A love for myself and for others, that I had never felt before …for anyone …for anything." In private, I told him that this peace was the result of chemical processes in the brain that are triggered before you die. According to scientific studies, before death one was filled with happiness and love for everyone. I believed that this was the result of millions of years of evolution so as to spare us any agony upon dying. He dismissed my view with the wave of a hand.

If something like that could be felt, I could not feel it.

CLASS N° 7

Nor could I imagine the nothingness as intended by Seymour's followers. Who could imagine something like that? I did not hear metaphysical explanations such as you read about in books by Heidegger. On the contrary, these theoretical explanations were the sickly inventions of Seymour Jørgensen's mind. First, one was to imagine himself walking along the shore of a river; then one was pushed to imagine that the "river" continued to exist even if you were not there to see it.

"Nothingness is absolute, it is the face of all things…" and while he talked I tried to imagine the world without me – but I could not.

LAST CLASS

I should imagine the beating of a dead heart.

One should imagine that the stopped heart, like that of Stephen's when he had the near death experience, was still beating. For a few minutes the sounds of jungle animals were reproduced by a unique recorder set up on a table in the front of the room. When Jørgensen turned off the recorder he asked us to imagine that the sounds were still there. According to this premise one died when his heart was no longer beating. While it continued to beat one was therefore alive.

***

These were the eight classes which Seymour Jørgensen intended to teach us how to "contemplate death and live to tell the tale."

The other typical facts of near death experiences were not included in these classes: seeing relatives already dead; or the experience of entering a tunnel with a distant light at its end.

This was my only contact with Seymour Jørgensen.

I stopped seeing Stephen and we took different paths in life.

CHESS GAMES

To José

Chess is not a game to sooth the spirit. For those who still play it is in front of the chessboard that, many a time, the worst aspect of each one of us comes to light.

Long ago some friends told me about a certain stranger they met in a train. According to this fellow, he had been a consummate chess player in his youth. "I even beat Najsdorf years ago. I have not always worked as a waiter." He was disqualified from several tournaments, which he attributed to jealousy, and then, had no other option but to work like a donkey from sunup to sundown to earn his daily bread. It is well known that chess which is not regularly practiced is easily forgotten. He let my friends know that he no longer knew what castling was. It was his way of telling them that they had ruined his life. Who were they?

Could you believe him? Whether true or not, such fellows enrich the abundant myths that surround the game. And there are many myths for sure.

Jose Sonsino, the famous chess player, played better than I did: out of five games, I won one – and I do not doubt that it was because my foolish persistence in playing repeatedly, without interruption, exhausted him. I tried all the variants, from a Caro-Kann to a classic King's Gambit, with the same adverse outcome. One night I jokingly said that his game was more refined than that of the Cuban, Capablanca. This raised in him a vague memory that he related to me with much detail. It was during the time when we studied together late at night.

"Ten years ago I met a fellow with whom I played correspondence chess. You know: one writes a letter with a move enclosed and the other responds in the same way. His last name was the same as one of the chess players you find in chess books, but his game was rudimentary, as bad as that of a beginner. We were playing for almost a year and a half before he finally accepted that I had defeated him. I told him, without intending to offend, that I was going to checkmate him in four moves. He finally understood that this was so. After a few months had passed he invited me to spend a weekend with him in his cottage far to the south. I accepted immediately. Perhaps both of us were curious to meet one another."

"How was he? A retired man about 65 or 70 years old, completely bald on the top of his head but with white hair falling like a theatre curtain from just above his ears to his shoulders. Does his physical description matter…? No, except to show he appeared normal at first sight. Soon after I arrived he opened a chess board on the table. He asked if I wanted to play white or black, and, sitting in front of me said: *we'll see if you can beat me now*."

"I asked him for a glass of water or a cup of tea, if he did not mind (I had travelled more than 500 kilometers after all). But he made a gesture of disgust with his hand and saying – first things first. We played and I won in less than half an hour at which point I said that my mouth was dry. The fellow stood up, went to get something from a desk, took a gun out of one of the drawers, and, pointing it at me, said: *we'll play another game. No tea. Keep playing or you'll have a hole in your head.* He moved back, sat down in front of me and with his free hand placed a chess clock on the table. *Games will be five minutes for each player. If you lose, I will kill you.*"

"But listen sir, I said, someone will hear the shot, at which point he fired into the ceiling. The echo rumbled in my ears. *No one will come, we are in the back of beyond.* And he repeated: *if you lose I will kill you, so play well.* Throughout the room chess trophies were displayed along with photographs of famous chess players from bygone years such as Lasker and shelves with books which seemed to be all about chess."

"Listen, I answered. Have you gone mad? And I made as if I was going to leave. He put the gun barrel to my face and told me: *listen, don't you understand? I will kill you. I will kill you!* He was so close to my face that the smell of garlic coming out of his mouth nauseated me. Drunk, he was not. I assure you."

"The second game I also won. *You think you are smart*, he whispered between the few teeth still left in his mouth. I won four more games at which point, suddenly, he took my queen, placed it on the side of the chessboard and told me: *now you will always play black and without the queen. We will see how well you play.* And I won again and again. In one of the games I almost lost by time, but I checkmated him with my knight and bishop so easily that his face turned beet red with shame."

"He took away one of my rooks, limiting himself to say: *and now?* He lost again. As I glanced sideways at all those trophies it occurred to me that this madman must surely believe himself to be the best chess player of his small town. And imagine – here I was – showing him that he was no better than a rookie."

"In those old wooden chess clocks the sound is very loud. It was my turn. I pressed the button down (I heard 'knock'); then his turn (I heard 'knock' again); and so on. I heard the sound of the button being pressed down on the clock over and over. My head was about to explode as the persistent sound upset me and, for that reason I moved faster and faster. Sometimes I heard 'knock-knock', 'knock-knock', repeatedly at least twenty or thirty times in ten seconds. But I always won."

"Then he took away the other rook asking me if I could beat him. I was about to lose each game when, in a foolish desire to win with quality he would suddenly make a wrong move and lose. I asked if we hadn't already played enough games. We have played for four hours, I said. Don't you realize that you can't beat me? Did he? That was too naïve on my part. He put the gun down on the table and took away one of my bishops and also one of my knights from the opposite side. So my pieces were simply: eight pawns, one knight, the king and one bishop against the complete 16 pieces of the fellow. I thought: Jose, you are about to die."

"What did I do? As expected, I played a defensive style. I moved all my pieces to the side and waited for that madman to attack me. He made sacrifices as if he were Spielmann, the man who wrote: 'The Art of Sacrifice in Chess'. Do you remember?"

"He gave away one of his rooks for one of my pawns, his queen for another, and, in a few more moves, we had the same quantity of pieces. Can you believe it? I was winning! The fellow was furious and began to hit the table with the butt of his gun. Be careful, I said, or you will shoot someone with it. *I will shoot someone! You – through the head*, he yelled. I don't know if it was fatigue but my eyes closed and I made a mistake such as could happen to anyone even though my life depended on me not doing so. But I grabbed my king without intending to do it."

"*Chess piece touched, chess piece moved*, he said strictly referring to the touch-move rule. I looked at the clock: only 30 seconds more remained and my time, not his, was running out. I could not think much about my next move as I had so little time left. The famous first match between Karpov and Kasparov came to my mind. It did not matter where I moved my king. I had lost. The fellow had finally won and I couldn't care less. I hit the clock to make his time pass. I stood up and shouted to his face: kill me if you want but you know nothing about playing chess."

"The fellow brandished the gun and then placed it on the table. His enormous eyes opened, his head bent back and his back arched and he died. He lay still on the chair, his arms swinging to and fro like a pendulum."

Surely Jose was pulling my leg. "Of course," I said, "you were saved by a miracle".

"It is not just that," Jose told me. "His time expired without him making his move. He had also lost his last match." He grimaced, then laughed loudly at me.

In later years Jose confessed to me that he had adapted his narrative from a story by Hemingway, although, up until now, I have read more than fifty of his stories and have yet to find it.

THE DEAD

Could there be anything more absurd than this – the unlikely fact of being alive in the here and now and not knowing why?"
Author's question for the readers of the story

On May 1, 2026, an extraordinary event occurred in a small town of ancient Japan and the news went around the world... Which town? Good question! Because after many vain and repeated efforts by some people, it did not even show as a black dot in any atlas. The local and national newspapers informed us of the following, as reported in "The Okinawa Times":

> **On the afternoon of April 30th Nariaki Takizawa died. One day later, as a religious ceremony was being officiated, he suddenly came back to life. It is said that he had stuck his head out of the open coffin which was**

surrounded by family members, his pale face still showing the pains of death, and asked: "Where am I?"

But can a dead man, Mr. Takizawa in this case come back to life having been dead almost a whole day? Scientists, commenting to the press, said that this was impossible. Neurons begin to die when the oxygen supply to the brain is blocked. According to them if one does not breathe for more than five minutes one dies immediately. Therefore, if one is dead, "scientifically dead" of course, one remains dead. The highest officials of the Church of Rome were more cautious; although they preferred not to dwell on this unlikely fact (and make mistakes), they did assert that miracles were possible. After all, did Jesus not come back to life three days after his death?

Overnight more newspapers were sold, more books about the paranormal published and a few people came closer to God. As for Takizawa, he died six months later and did not rise the next day, nor in 3 days, nor in 7 days. His tombstone became a curiosity before which tourists had their pictures taken with its inscription:

$$1942 - 30/04/2026$$
$$01/05/2026 - 07/11/2026$$

For reference on what he said about the hereafter read: "Nariaki Takizawa, The First Dead Among the Living" by Brad Pitt. It was vox populi that his death had been misdiagnosed; Poe's tales about premature burials as well as profusely detailed historical sources were cited.

On December 2, the same year, other newspapers reported the following cases: a woman from the Samoan Islands and an American cowboy came back to life on the same day although not at the same hour. What if it had been the same hour? And if it was the same time and the first digit was the same as a number such as e, π, or √2, then even the most stubborn scientist would have had to budge and admit that there was in fact a cosmic order hidden behind a veil after all.

Both of these resurrected persons asserted, as Mr. Takizawa in turn had done, that they did not remember anything at all of what had happened after dying. "It was like not having existed, and suddenly – life again," wrote the American cowboy in his memoirs. Soon, however, and against all logic, the cases came to be numbered in the thousands, and that from one city alone. There was one who said he was the resurrection of Elvis Presley and another who called himself Spinoza, the latter being an example of the "cultured dead" for who knows a whit about Spinoza these days? Of course these were fraudulent cases which were designed to make large sums of money. It was true that it was good business to come back to life after dying. The cowboy from Ohio bought a luxurious mansion; he was making a pile of money and for what reason? Only for showing his face on TV while explaining nothing. Science divided these cases into two types: a) the veridical and b) the opportunistic. The former already counted a hundred cases as death was determined to have occurred hours or one or two days earlier. Otherwise there could be no resurrection. Christians spoke of "The Judgement of the Great Day", in which even the oceans would give back the dead (refraining from explaining how the dead would have to swim to shore). These cases were from the here and now it should be emphasized, the "fresh dead" from a few days ago, or the "newly dead" as some said.

In three months alone there were as many dead as alive – a humorous expression of course, nothing else. The dead were eating and drinking the same as any of us. And dressed in ordinary clothes, they did not differ from the living at all. According to the superstitious, whose opinions should not be taken into account, their eyes had an unnatural glassy glow.

Kin could not believe that their parents had risen. "And to think he was dead!" became a common statement. Scientists could not explain the phenomenon. Among the educated, T. Crown, an eminent psychiatrist, spoke of how that which we had so much desired (to live forever or for at least a few more years), had finally become a reality in this century.

An assassinated president occupied his position again and asserted that both the living and the "newly dead" would have the same rights before the law. Nothing could be more false. Many factories posted this sign: "WE DO NOT HIRE THE DEAD". But how could one know who were the living and who were the dead? As I said earlier, it was claimed that the dead's eyes had a glassy glow. But was this definite proof? My eyes have a glassy glow and I have not died yet.

At this point, it would be appropriate to digress and

mention the twice dead, the three times dead, 4, 5 and so the list goes on. Some claimed to have died many times and that this had been happening since the time of Nefertiti. Whether this was true or they were betting on the ignorance of people no one can say. It could be true. I base this assertion on the fact that many religious people, by their own hands, often murdered in cold blood those dead who came back to life and whose very existence they found offensive for refuting their ancient beliefs.

Cases were overflowing by their large numbers. The daily newspapers quoted a rich man who, after dying, wished to cancel his will. Could he have it annulled even though it had been executed after his death? His own wife asserted that he had died and that his fortune was now hers. And his son tried to kill him again so as to collect the inheritance. As for the dead who were poor, it was mentioned that the rooms to resettle them were small. Who had not counted on the death of a loved one providing more space at home?

The dead became pariahs. Many were not accepted back into their own families. It was good to have them back for a while but after that it was wished that they go back to the place from which they had come. The living held public demonstrations with banners that said: "Go away!" or "DEAD – NO!!!" Who owed anything to the dead after all! A scientist suggested sending them to Mars but revoked his own proposal after having a cardiac arrest and returning to life two days later. Perhaps we are not impartial in our judgements. The dead were among the living and there was no telling the difference between them. The shock and bewilderment this caused brought out the worst in human beings.

And if someone who had died then married someone living and they had a son, what was he: half dead or half alive? The wisest among us did not know. The most superstitious christened them "zombies." The term prospered even though it was incorrect as the "newly dead", or "half alive", or "zombies" were as alive as any of us. The inventiveness of man is unlimited. To cite some of the craziest examples: restaurants with names such as "The New Zombie" or "Je Suis un Zombie"; or sportswear stores such as "Zombie Sport"; or toy stores for zombie children called "Zombies R Us", or books (some of them bestsellers) with titles like "10 Rules to Not Look Like a Zombie"; or esoteric ones such as "The Zombie Alchemist". And there were, of course, beds for zombies, forks, toothpaste, toilets, and even fans and dye for zombie hair. Scientifically, and this was repeated thousands of times ad nauseum by newspapers, TV news and even at public events, we and "zombies" were equals.

Mankind increased by 35 percent in a few months and, due to overpopulation, governments enacted laws with an unheard of speed to deal with the situation. Basically all countries agreed on the following law: "Every family must take care of its own dead". There were those who asked for a discount on taxes and increased benefits so that a family with two dead would get twice the subsidy compared to a family with only one dead; if it had three, then three times the benefit and so on. The logic of this, wrong as it was, led to "orphanages of the dead" being opened, which collected money, giving back a small proportion in return for room and board. Many of these places were pigsties. A mother of quintuplets said of her family: "I wish they had been stillborn". In this bonanza of bad behaviour were the gravediggers who offered promotions: bury the dead, two for one; or full price for the first of the dead, half price for the second; or two dead in the same coffin (while pointing out that it didn't matter whether the coffin was a crate for apples or one fit for a king since the dead would, in a few hours or days, come back to life). Being buried became a luxury for the few. Many people no longer buried the dead; they put up with the foul smell while at the same time claiming benefits from the government.

Some burials were prohibited by law. It was enough to imagine someone buried underground coming back to life and having no means of escape.

Vendettas became as obsolete as the abacus. Why kill someone only to have them come back and kill you the next day? Finally people began to forgive the faults of others. If you were slapped on the cheek you simply turned the other one.

Suicide ceased to be newsworthy. A case became public of a young Greek, Dexteropolus, who claimed to have killed himself a thousand times. In a television interview he said: "At first I cut my veins; later I shot myself; I bled to death or died from freezing." All for the purpose of publicizing his book: "1001 Ways to Commit Suicide with Bon Goût".

Those who were begging in the street had a saying: "I am dead. Nobody will hire me – spare change." The dead had their own religion. A new one, invented recently in the West was "The Church of the Dead Christians." There were those, basing themselves on the biblical verse "let the dead bury their dead," who said that everything was in the Bible. Some wanted to add to that, everything from dinosaurs to satellites. "Come back to the fold my lost souls," were the words of the preacher R. "d" Parker (the lowercase "d" meaning dead). But could both be accepted as truths: religion and the events of recent months. Yes, if you followed the premise of Luther: "Interpret the Bible in any way you see fit."

Countries did not allow the dead of other countries to pass through their borders particularly their airports. Who would be responsible for the costs? Several countries went to war over this –resettle to what end? None. With more dead (casualties from these wars) and more benefits being claimed, politicians resorted to diplomacy, lies and blackmail so as to get rid of their dead. Many countries accepted the dead of others in exchange for a reduction in their international debt. The rate for each 1,000 dead was a debt reduction of 0.05 percent. Thus, if 20,000 dead were accepted the debt was reduced by 1 percent. (And yes, the dead were also listed on the stock market!).

Animals, once dead did not come back to life. Some eccentrics implored one or another deity to bring his or her puppy back to life. A billionaire went further, offering half of his fortune to buy food for the poor if God (whoever he was) would return his pet lizard alive to him again. He even promoted a foundation called "HELP TITUS". Titus was obviously the name of the animal. Pranksters wrote captions under the name of Titus that were both absurd and distasteful. Others, I remember, made comments such as: "How many would eat with even one-tenth of that half fortune!" But, of course, everyone knows what to do with what is his or hers in this fair world.

And scientists? To be honest, their impartiality ended when their families came back to life. What more scientific proof was needed! And, although there were those who had no one who had died and come back to life and denied everything, their arguments were banal. They claimed that people were prey to collective hallucinations, or that the whole concept of the dead coming back to life was totally unscientific.

Hospitals became "a thing of the past." This was demonstrated by the lunatic cancer patient who shot himself and was resurrected – healed. So who needed a hospital? In them sick patients were murdered. Then there was a wait of a few days and they came back alive. Murder methods were refined par excellence: the guillotine was a favorite, back again and in vogue. Many resorted to rat poison although the more educated chose Socrates' hemlock. Governments paid an exorbitant sum to those that did not kill themselves and who spent a few weeks interned in a hospital. Hospitals that closed were turned into museums with the slogan: "Here operations were done." So were the little ones taught. All the diseases that once decimated humanity now became legends on the same level as dragons or the Loch Ness monster.

Public demonstrations gradually disappeared. The banners "Go away!" or "Die again!" or "The world belongs to the living", were no longer seen. If something becomes part of daily life you get used to it, even accept it.

Mr. Takizawa returned to the living and it is said (as

reported by "The Okinawa Times") that he laughed out loud when he saw his tombstone. When the dead who had died in the past several weeks came back to life, governments ordered that all the dead be unearthed. They even asked medical practitioners to return the bones purchased from cemeteries. Some of those who came back to life spoke of the ordeal of being locked in too narrow a coffin. Others, after returning to life, died again from lack of oxygen. With all those who were unearthed the cities could not cope with so many souls. But somehow we made room for them because they were also part of our modern world.

And life, as hard as it was, went on with the dead, the living and the zombies (if I may use that outmoded word).

The afternoon had been stormy in Bellfountain even though its sad autumns are no longer blessed as often with rain. The tenuous glimmer of the red sun fading into the distant horizon came crawling through the attic window allowing me to see the many cobwebs scattered at the back of the room. The light bathed, with a reddish hue, the things forgotten there, giving them a ghostly appearance. When walking to a chair that rested on a corner, I remembered the countless afternoons spent reading books that were now silent and abandoned to their fate under a pile of ancient dust.

I heard the rocking chair creak, ending its dreaming as I sat upon it; my attitude was as heretical as it was mundane, because there are things that should not be disturbed from their monotonous silence when the dust of oblivion has already claimed them for its inheritance. As I listened a multitude of distant murmurs reminded me of the seduction of fugitive afternoons from my childhood. I stayed there for a while watching something that was sleeping in shadows of a corner: an old oil lamp amongst the other oddities that were kept there. By the dim light of this relic of the past I liked to read books. I do not know why. Turning my head I saw something on a table hidden behind a thick layer of dust and fragments of dry paint fallen from the ceiling.

It was an open book, its cover worn out by years of quiet, waiting under a roof through which an intrusive rain was dripping lacerating its yellowed pages. As I got up it seemed as if thousands of imaginary beings, hidden behind otherworldly veils, accompanied me moving in the presence of he who had played with them here a long time ago. I got closer to the book and moved my hand over its pages. The rain did not touch it. It was just an optical illusion due to the dim light. My hand swept a century of dust off the pages of the book where it had been left open. It was the grimoire that I read at the age of ten or twelve which my grandfather had given me to introduce myself into the mysteries of occultism.

OUROBOROS

Still hid in mist, and on the left
Went down into the sea.
The Rime of the Ancient Mariner, Part 11,
Samuel Taylor Coleridge

From Monday to Friday the 5 (Avenue Road) bus of the Toronto Transit Commission passes by the corner of Cottingham Street at 3:15 PM. In approximately seven minutes, it takes you to within a few meters of the Museum subway station, named for the Royal

Ontario Museum which is located opposite it.

The bus trip is direct, just 6 stops. At the first one of these stops, late in the evening on Saturdays, a couple of families with many children usually get on – followers of Hare Krishna whose temple is right there. At the stop by Davenport Road, an area known for its cafes, flower and antique shops, some lovers (if it is not too cold) will board on Sunday afternoons. At the next two stops it is rare to see anyone getting either on or off. Next is Yorkville: here a lot of people get off as they are going to work, or get on as they are returning home. The following stop is Bloor Street, a few blocks from the chic part of Toronto. The sixth stop is Museum. Here everyone gets off along with myself. These passengers have been with me since I had boarded the bus at Cottingham Street.

What caught my attention the first time I saw him? I wonder, especially since in this city no one gives a damn about the lives of others. Everyone does whatever they please as is it more and more the case in our modern times. Still, I repeatedly looked sideways at him as if we were the alpha and omega of a shared destiny.

The old man held my grandfather's grimoire in his hands, the same one which at the same time I pressed against my knees with my sweaty hands. The corners of the cover, both top and bottom, were bent by years of reading. The spine of the book was broken; its pages about to come off. The brown cover, dried and cracked by the sun, seemed as insignificant as a plot of land in the Congo lacerated by decades of drought. At the bottom edge (which the old man purposely allowed me to notice), my first name could be read, just as I had written it on my own book last fall. It was a copy of my grimoire but one that looked to have been in the world for almost a hundred years. Who could this old man be, sitting there at the front of the bus, other than a practitioner of occultism, a sorcerer or a summoner of demons? Two minutes later I got off at the Museum subway station and, without looking back, ran for the stairs.

That year (I turned 13 a few months after the incident), I swore that if I saw him again I would not behave as cowardly as that first time. In the first five of the seven minutes that the driver would take from Cottingham Street to the Museum subway station my hands would sweat, my breathing become agitated, and my heart gallop as if it were trying to escape from my chest. A couple of people would get on or off but the old man never did. Nor did he wait at the bus stop and, as I fantasized, let the bus go without taking it because he saw me. I did not see him until three years later. He immediately noticed my presence as I had noticed his.

Even at the age of fifteen we are still like children, trying to find a supernatural explanation for everything. Then the later years make us into materialists, atheists, nihilists, cynics, attached to the desire to make a career or fortune as if we were never going to die. Forgive me if I do not believe that science can provide us with a faith, already dead, that can give salvation to man. What would that salvation be: that of some numbers written by the rickety and squalid hands of those who no longer believe in anything?

At fifteen, then, I saw him again... should I have

done something? Yes, as I had promised I would. As I stood up to go to the front of the bus to see him, the old man suddenly opened my grandfather's grimoire (as the incident to follow confirmed) and held it open for my eyes to see. It was the page with the ouroboros which caused me to return to my seat with my head down. A few minutes later, I got off at the Museum subway station and, just as I had the first time, ran for the stairs without looking back.

The ouroboros appeared as drawn on a page of my grandfather's grimoire. Later on I knew it to be a copy of the drawing published in De Lapide Philosophico Triga Chemicum, Prague 1599 by the Frenchman Nicolas Barnaud who was known in the alchemical circles of the time. Why that drawing? Why? In the following years I thoroughly researched the meaning of the serpent or dragon biting its own tail and believe me, I could make neither head nor tail of it.

Then came my college years: I was determined to make a career in the world as a philologist. A few months after turning 20 I saw the old man again just as he was getting off at the Museum station. Two things had changed about him: his right arm was in a cast held at 90 degrees by a sling; and second his face was that of a younger man than I had first seen eight years ago. It was for that reason that I doubted that it could be the same person that had held the grimoire. He was not even looking at me; haggard as if he had spent sleepless nights, his eyes were fixed on the floor of the bus.

Six months later I was almost 21. So much snow fell that year that I wondered if it would ever stop. I noticed him as soon as I got on the bus at Cottingham

Street. I walked past him. It was true: the fellow was younger. His face was like that of my grandfather's. I convinced myself that I should ask him what his job was. As he got off at College Street, two stops beyond Museum, I followed him shouting: "Hey, wait a second, I must speak with you." He stumbled and fell on the sidewalk after which he took a taxi. Before he disappeared I put my hands on the window and looked him straight in the eye. What did I see in his eyes but the color of mine. He left without bothering to explain who he was. Perhaps he was afraid? Then over the years I came to realize he was not. There was a more compelling reason for him not to meet me. (Fool of me not to think about the ouroboros at that time!) I also knew that when he fell that day he had fractured the same arm that had been previously broken.

To finish my doctoral thesis and when I was 22, I travelled to the countries of the Old World. When I was in town I lived with a friend for which reason my trips on the 5 bus became part of history. Except for once, when I visited my parents for a farewell party and stayed overnight. The next morning I took the 5 bus for the first time in almost three years. There was the old man sitting on the bus. I doubted that it was an accident – it was too much of a coincidence. It was July 3. I could not forget the date because the next day I was to leave for Spain and not return for 10 years. The fellow was much younger, rejuvenated with each encounter. He looked to be about 45 or 50 (later I knew that he was 47). We looked at each other for the entire trip without saying a word. Strange as it may seem, we were the only two passengers throughout the trip. He reminded me of my grandfather (as I remembered him when I was a child) and, if you can believe me, also of myself but 20 years older.

The first year of my return from Europe, and when I was 36, it happened that I saw myself twice on the same day on the number 5 bus. I took it on a Saturday morning as usual because the stop was only a few meters from my parents' house with whom I was living temporarily. He was sitting at the back. I just kept thinking it must be an abracadabra with the old man faking my face. What should I do: go ask him if he was me? The second time, in the afternoon, I took the bus the bus a couple of stops earlier and sat at the back. A fellow, identical to me got on at Cottingham Street, noticed my presence and sat at the front.

We never touched and I realize now that this could not be. For what would happen to the world if we did?

I did not see the old man ever again. Perhaps he was dead, or no longer taking the 5 bus. Or had his schedule suddenly changed? Or...who knows? Then, a couple of years later, there was the year I got sick and was in bed for nearly six months. There were many more excuses that would justify why we did not meet.

But the mind still reasons even when we are asleep.

Then, at the age of 47 I saw him on the bus. The old man? No, the young man. We looked at each other for the entire trip without exchanging a word. Strange as it may seem, for the entire trip we were the only passengers. He reminded me of myself before my trip to Europe, except 20 years younger. The young man looked at me, his eyes threatening the world and destiny. This much was unalterable; I was unable to go to his side and touch him.

That winter, when I was 51, I took the precaution

of boarding the 5 bus a couple of stops earlier. I was sure that I was going to see that young man again, and also, that we should not meet at the same bus stop. That winter it snowed as heavily as it had 30 years earlier. I noticed him as soon as he got on the bus at Cottingham Street. I walked past him. It was true; the fellow was younger. His face was like mine at the age of 21. I knew he would follow me when I got off at College Street. He shouted to my back: "Hey, wait a second, I must speak with you." I stumbled and fell on the sidewalk after which I took a taxi. Before I disappeared he put his hands on the window and looked me straight in the eye. What did I see in his eyes but the color of mine? I left without bothering to explain who I was. Perhaps he would believe me if I explained to him who I was? Could I have explained it to him? Of course not. That day I broke my arm when I fell.

I knew that I would meet him again and six months later I saw him but led him to believe I had not. He had not closed his eyes all night as he had tried to decipher this delirium. The sling was still holding my arm at 90 degrees.

The boy would be 15 years old…what if he did something? Yes, he promised himself that he would. He stood up and went to the front of the bus to see me. He stopped suddenly when I opened my grandfather's grimoire and held it open for his eyes to look at. It was the page with the ouroboros. Seeing it he went back to his seat and put his head down. A few minutes later he got off at the Museum subway station. As I had, those many years ago, he ran for the stairs without looking back.

I always wondered if cutting my hand would break the symmetry. I never dared to do so nor did I take that bus as often in case I should find the boy once again. As it was logical to close the circle I saw him again when I was 60. I held the grimoire as I had the first time he saw me. I let him see his first name on the cover, now even more cracked by the sun. Looking at it he must have thought that I was a practitioner of occultism.

The serpent (or was it a dragon?) bit its tail. I did some drawings on paper to clarify my confused ideas. The first arrow is the life of the young man; the second one, that of the old man:

$$12 - 15 - 20 - 21 - 25 - 36 \rightarrow$$
$$\leftarrow 60 - 57 - 52 - 51 - 47 - 36$$

One of these days I think I should go to the Department of Applied Mathematics and ask if something like this could be true. But what would I say? What scientific evidence could I present that would make my story true?

There are certainly many mysteries that are impossible for the human mind to comprehend. If my theory is true I will die at the point when I turn 72. On the other hand, if I am still alive, I will laugh my head off at this quirk of my destiny.

So now what? I will sit and wait…

Who is Thomas Ligotti?

16 YEARS

1. THE FACTS

The facts are very simple:

1. A student of mine,
2. 16 years old,
3. committed suicide,
4. just after midnight on Monday, February 24, this year,
5. by hanging himself from one of the beams of the ceiling of his own room,
6. which was completely dark.

Six facts described in as few words as necessary because that is how it happened.

One wonders... how did he hang himself if the room was completely dark? How did he find the chair to climb onto, then the rope to hang himself by? And finally how did he see, to slip the noose over his head, to tighten the knot and then kick the chair away leaving himself hanging stiff from one of the beams of the ceiling? Perhaps one could venture that the light of a wan moon hitting him full in the face could explain these facts rationally. Perhaps it was the light of a vagabond dying moon which in addition to his face also lit up the room allowing him to see the chair, the rope and the knot. But was it not true that the moon was already hidden below the horizon at that early hour on Monday and that the room was completely dark?

His parents were forty something.

The father was a psychologist. He gave the misleading impression of being older because of the bald spot on the crown of his head that could only be seen from above. He brought to mind Pythagoras, as depicted in the painting *Scuola di Atene* by Rafael. Or maybe I'm wrong? At first he tried to hide it with artificial hair, sprayed on so that when it dried it looked, by color and texture, like real hair.

The mother, who rarely wore makeup or gave any importance to clothes, was obsessed with shoes. She wore her hair in the style of Annette Bening in the film "My Dear President" (though she would not have liked to hear that comparison) and earrings in the shape of an Ankh or Crux Ansata. Her green eyes were as delicate in color as that of freshly cut grass. She was a teacher of chemistry in the school where we both taught.

As a family they led a good life that, without being rich, allowed them to travel the world: to the minarets of Hagia Sofia, the old fortifications of San Angelo on the shores of Malta and more remote places (Mombasa, Siem Riep, Luang Prabang, the Baron Bliss Lighthouse in Belize city), of which little or nothing is known.

The boy was an only child. Since he was the best at his school no one had any doubt that, whatever his chosen profession, he would go farther in life than his parents. As far as Bill Gates or Sergey Brin…? An exaggerated statement, perhaps, but that reflected a reality that could be. Finally, and maybe it matters little (or not at all), he was seen as someone who lived behind a stone wall. He brought to mind the memory of Bob Geldof hitting that wall in the film "Pink Floyd, The Wall". He was a *rara avis* if, at that young age, the expression could be used to describe him. His classmates, not knowing it, called him "Martian" which as nicknames go meant the same thing. It was not known whether he had friends or a girlfriend. He was quiet and, although he did not keep himself apart from others, he was often seen alone with a sad or melancholy face like that of Lord Byron in the portrait by Le Brun; as if life were pushing him down and burying him alive, as one of his classmates said. In the two years he was my student I remember he asked me a couple of irrelevant questions that I would never have interpreted as indicating he was making a decision to take his own life.

Although I did not know him privately, when I was told what had happened, I simply could not believe it. Later, analyzing the facts *a posteriori*, I said to myself, that of all my students, he was the one that "sooner or later would commit suicide." (I repeat these are reflections reached *a posteriori*, after calmly analyzing the facts).

At the wake, which I attended out of obligation more than anything else, I was told of the events that summed up the last minutes of the boy's life: the same sequence of six facts in almost the same number of words. It goes without saying that no one understood why he had done it. His mother, as she kept lamenting, repeated again and again that she had not realized that something was happening to her son. She said that, as a present, he had been given a trip to England to see his favorite rock and roll band in March (she did not say which one). He had asked his parents for that trip a few months ago. On the weekend, after months of preparation, he told his parents he would not be going without explaining why. Then he closed the door of his room. It was the last time he was seen alive.

A month after the wake, the suicide of the 16 year old boy came up in a conversation I had with another one of his teachers. She did not refer to the boy or his reasons for killing himself. Everyone seemed to agree there could be none. Instead she said of his mom, "The mother is desperate: she wonders why her son killed himself." He left no suicide note. He said nothing to anyone. If the boy did not say anything… then how could we know? She asked me if I knew anything. I told her I did not.

One day in late April about two months after the suicide the boy's mother passed me in the school hallway. It brought to mind Jung's theory of synchronicity: where facts that seem to have no relationship to one another happen to appear as if one were the cause of the other. I decided not to bother her with questions that had probably been asked many times and which were of a private nature which she certainly would not want to share with me. I opted for a casual greeting which, as in all of these situations, began with me talking about the weather.

"What crazy weather!" I said.

"Yes. First rain, then the sun appears, then cold and rainy again. What madness!" she told me.

It was a conversation that would not add anything to anyone's life. I hid the book by Camus that I was reading and which I promised myself I would finish. Suddenly she asked: "Are you still interested in Buddhism?" I said I was not, accompanying my words with a shake of my head and briefly explaining my reasons.

"I have being an atheist all my life," she said, "since I was born if that is possible." The words came out of her mouth as mechanically as if reading a book aloud. "An atheist would wonder: where was God when my son was killing himself? Who is this God but a murderer? To kill and to allow someone to die without lifting a finger to prevent it are the same thing. But now I do not know what to think. There is something that is not right…" I just nodded my head and squinted showing interest in what she said to me just as I had when I re-read one of the first stories by Borges trying to understand what was written.

"In the morning I went looking for my son to wake him up to go to school. I will never be able to erase from my head the image of him hanging from one of the ceiling beams at 6:30 on that Monday. I saw him" (she said putting her hand on her chest); "You," (the same hand now pointing at my chest); "You did not. Nor was it your son who killed himself." I did not think she was attacking me or blaming me for her son's death. I was his teacher after all. I believe that she was unburdening herself to me. Or even, as some of us do, thinking aloud to find an explanation for an absurd fact.

"Why did he do it? He left no note. No words of reproach (if only he could have done so). Never in my life would I have thought that he could do something like that…"

She paused and asked, "Is my son dead? Is he really dead? I speak not of his body, but of his consciousness, of that which he was, of that which we are, of our soul if you will. I know you are saying to yourself, 'but isn't it she who does not believe in God, or the soul, or anything supernatural.' And you would be right: I do not believe. But I have to keep living, I have to find a reason to breathe… every day, one more minute, one more second. What good is all the money in the world, my work, travelling to Europe if I do not have him…? I need something to give me hope, something to believe in."

After a while she left, without another word, smiling. A distant smile, dying hopeless on her wet lips.

I learned from other teachers, friends of mine, that while the father continued his work as a psychologist as if nothing had happened, the mother had been attending the places of worship of diverse religions. She herself told a friend she was reading about Taoism, perhaps in the ying and yang was the ultimate truth. On Saturday nights she was attending the temple of the Open Brethren. I know that they are Christians but not much more than that. On Sundays she went to

Mass. And she always carried under her arm the book "Reasons and Persons" by the British philosopher Derek Parfit (which I tried to find so I could read it, but in vain).

At first glance it seems that the image of her son hanging from one of the beams had made her go mad. She that had mocked God, religion, and superstition as things of the past and mocked all those who believed that there was something more than what our eyes could see. What would be next? Preaching the gospel at street corners...? Singing "My Sweet Lord" as George Harrison did? Seeing is believing say the old women living a long life.

2. SUBSEQUENT EVENTS

On June 12 of this year the mother was found dead: hanging from the same beam of the ceiling of her son's room and, although it is perhaps speculation, died at more or less the same time of a Monday morning. Her husband informed the police that his wife had begun acting increasingly crazy in recent months. (I have to believe that he did not refer to madness in the vague sense but rather that she exhibited erratic behaviour, a sickly obsession and expressed bizarre ideas.) Unlike her son, she left a note. There were a handful of meaningless words that explained neither her suicide nor that of her son's. Although I do not know for sure as I never saw the note, according to those who did it said: *I'm going to look for...* (name of her son which I omit for obvious reasons). *I do not expect to return.* These two sentences were in the mouths of all who knew her. For some...

what could be more proof that she had gone crazy?

One afternoon, just before she killed herself, the mother came across me again, I believe by chance. She looked haggard as if she had not slept for several days. She then repeated the same talk and, as much as I can remember, with almost the same words as in the discussion we had two months after her son's suicide. I could understand none of it.

Finally, upset by her own words she said: "My son knew more than all of you... the wise ones... scientists," she spat. "It disgusts me, those of you who think that you know everything, when in fact you know nothing. Do you understand me? You know nothing. Nothing at all. Nothing. My son was the only one who found the way. My little son."

I interrupted: "Your son killed himself. He found no other way out. Death is not a solution. Whatever reason he may have had for not continuing to live his suicide was an act of cowardice..." Immediately I regretted using that word. No death is cowardly. If chosen it is an act of heroism not the act of a coward. You have to be very brave to hang yourself from a beam of the ceiling in the room where you sleep every night.

She laughed uproariously at my words, spittle flying from between her teeth. She repeated: "You understand nothing" over and over again until she disappeared into the distance.

I still wonder: Why did she kill herself? I think, after having thought over and over again about the two suicides, that we will never know what happened. I will take these doubts to my own grave. I tell myself over and over again that this is so – we will never know.

And forgive me, for this statement comes from someone who thinks he knows everything.

Who is Thomas Ligotti?

PEBBLE IN A SANDBOX

It was an afternoon of one of the last days of August. Between 3 and 4. I do not know exactly because I no longer measure the passing of time by clocks except for the few that I might see in the tower of a railway station or the bijouterie stores that abound on certain avenues. The sky was so pristine that one could forgive everything. It was such a uniform blue color that I could swear my eyes were lying to me. And only far away noises could be heard, but very distant as if the city, a block away, was exiling itself leaving behind a handful of vehicles to scurry away in haste.

For no particular reason I stared at a pebble that had been thrown into the side of the sandbox at the park. Perhaps it was a quirk of fate but it seemed that my eyes had been obsessed by that specific pebble as I sat on one of the park benches. The persistent summer wind, which seem determined to make me close my eyes and which pushed my hair over my face, failed to make me fix my eyes upon another pebble, or on some trees or on other benches. Nor were my eyes clouded when I was preyed by *déjà vu*.

My son was playing in the sandbox. He went to a spout that was but a rusty straight tube protruding from the side of a circular concrete fountain. Two metal doors secured by a padlock were only open in the summer so that children could play. When the days were not so hot they only had that pipe to bring water to the sandbox and build their modest sandcastles. As he came back, holding in his hands a small plastic jar, he left a trail of water between the fountain and the sandpit.

Beside me was a woman advanced in years but who, I did not doubt, might still be having a love affair. She was playing with her granddaughter, speaking in a language that seemed familiar but which I did not understand. I guessed that it might be similar to Russian, from one of the countries that had formerly been under Soviet occupation. I thought maybe Albanian, as I had seen many refugees from Albania in the area. But one never knows. Both grandmother and granddaughter had the rough faces of farmers as described by Turgenev in his stories.

What could I say about that afternoon? That it was leaving without trouble or fanfare. Just another afternoon of a day when, in just half an hour, I would meet my wife. We would then walk along part of what is called in Toronto the Beltline Trail bordering Chaplin Crescent between Davisville subway station and Spadina Avenue. Probably the sun was hiding among the trees as it began to set but I was not paying any attention to it. The afternoon had the dull glow of autumn when it follows hot on the heels of summer. It was hot, but not too much so. It was the best time to take the children out to play – neither too hot nor too cold.

Suddenly a point of light began shining in the sky as if radiating from that of a half dozen suns. I hid my eyes behind my fingers so that it did not blind me and ran quickly over to my son and covered his eyes with my other hand. I figured it must be a nova, as astronomers call them, a star that explodes in the far reaches of the firmament. Or perhaps it was a meteorite hitting the moon and we would all die without issue? Or perhaps it was an atomic bomb exploding over Toronto? A spectral and, at the same time an unnatural light, was reflected in the trees. Their leaves were bathed in a violet hue, or a mixture of orange and violet. That is all I could see. In a few minutes the light faded away and in a few minutes more everything returned to normal.

I stared at the pebble again. I could describe it for those requiring further explanation. It was light brown in color. It would have blended into the skin of my arm if it were not for the multitude of spots similar to moles but of a different color. Among them, precisely highlighted, were some that did have the same dark color of moles. It was oval shaped, about 3 to 4 cm. long and 2 cm. wide. What was it? It did not seem to me to be a stone born in the depths of the earth millions of years ago. So what was it?

As I looked at it a first and last name, unknown to me, came to the tip of my tongue. I could swear that they were the names of a man who had touched the stone a few weeks ago. I knew the day and hour this had occurred. The man had picked it up unhurriedly with his right hand, caressing it at first. Later he weighed it to kill time and then, without much meditation, had thrown it aside to where it now rested.

For a second I was reminded of someone dying in bed, though not that of a hospital. I knew the names of the doctor and nurse who had visited him, the street where his house was and the day, hour and second of his death. I knew how many people had gone to his funeral and the words spoken at it by the priest. I knew the day when one of his children, now an old man, visited his tombstone for the last time. Were these past events or those of days and years not lived yet?

I knew that the pebble had been here for almost three years without anyone noting its existence. I knew that a child had touched it for a few seconds. I knew who the child was and where he lived. I knew. I had always known. I will always know. I do not know how to explain it any better. I knew that before the child had touched it a stray dog had sniffed at it and then urinated to one side. I could find that dog if I wished so. I knew where it was right now or was I just imagining that it was laying in an alley by Jarvis and Wellesley? That night it rained cats and dogs. The sound was like that of water from a shower hitting our heads while we covered our ears with our hands. It was the sound of an ancient rain, banal, leaving the echo of a vestigial memory.

I knew the names of the people who brought these stones (that pebble and others) to this park. I knew when they had done so and at what time they had eaten lunch and at what time they left. I knew where they lived and who their wives, children and friends were. I knew how much they were paid and the number on the cheques they received for the work they had done. I knew the names and addresses of the banks where the cheques were deposited and when the banks were built. I knew the license number of the truck used to carry the stones here. I also knew which country the pebble came from and from what region. I knew all of this in the same way I know how to breathe – without even thinking about it.

I went further back in time to when there were neither humans, nor dinosaurs, nor trilobites, to when the pebble was part of the magma of the Earth. I knew when and how it had formed. I felt the cold of antediluvian nights. I knew how many atoms the pebble had and how they were linked to one another. I could feel the force of attraction as when I connected the opposite poles of a magnet. That force sent a tingling through the fingers of the hand that held the pebble.

I knew that the knowledge of all of this would take me to the Big Bang – to the first imaginable instant after the Creation. I would then know how the world was created and why. Does God exist? Would I see him face to face? I turned my head away, stupefied by knowledge for which I was not prepared.

Then I went into the future – and quickly. Centuries, millennia, hundreds of millennia passed in the blink of an eye. I saw creatures similar to crabs (not clearly but as if wrapped in a thick fog) walking around this place that was no longer a park. It was as hot and dry as the Gobi desert. The sun blazed in a sky that was not ours. It was redder than that of a sunset and the clouds appeared as furrowed rows, as if they were being plowed. One of the creatures pushed the pebble to one side as it kept going towards an unknown destination. I knew when that creature would die. What right did I have to know what was yet to be? I turned my head and smiled as would a drunkard seeing a still half-full bottle of wine in front of his eyes.

I stared at the woman again. I knew her whole life. I knew the nickname she had been given by her parents when she had just turned six years of age. I felt that my skull would burst like an over-inflated balloon. When a tangle of facts and dates came into my head I thought it must be some form of telepathy. First the dates and then what had happened on those dates:

(October 1950, a kiss on wet lips); (1951); (1957); (March 15, at 10:15 an umbrella breaks while it is raining); (2018, the room is cold, the curtains sway, I am feeling cold, I am dying…)

Then more rapidly a series of static images lasting half a minute:

(someone sleeping); (snow on the street); (a park bench); (a broken walnut); (boiling water…)

And gradually I began to understand who this woman was. I knew her name, age, the language that she spoke and the country where she was born. I knew the names of her parents, her children and her two grandchildren of which the girl playing with my son was the youngest. I was ashamed to see the first kiss on her wet lips that someone gave her in October of

1950; I got wet in the rain that morning of March 15 when her umbrella broke and I was with her when she died alone in her bed in 2018. If I wanted I could go back in the past or forward into the future. I knew who her grandparents were and what type of wood her coffin would be made of. Everything was in present time.

The woman was screaming as she sank her hands into her dyed hair. She jumped about as if she were crazy. She could not stop laughing for a reason that defied comprehension. I tried to help her, to reach her, to take her in my arms and tell her that everything was fine. But I could not because I too was jumping like crazy and laughing and unable to stop without knowing why. I raised my eyes to the afternoon sky several times, spreading my arms and crying out, "now I understand." But now, what I understood at the time I do not know.

The two nurses who straightjacketed and quickly took me from the park said I cried out, "I know, I know." I told them that my son was playing. I learned later that my wife had arrived and looked after him. They said that I shouted at them, "You do not understand, I forgive you," and then again. "You do not understand".

It was not a dream. And then, like this, the incident occurred…

Who is Thomas Ligotti?

IT IS THUS PROVED

These three handwritten pages were excluded from the case by court order. It should be noted that they were not a defining influence at the time of sentencing. From these pages cross-outs have been removed and marginal notes and paragraphs have been added, where appropriate, to clarify the narrative. The original had only one paragraph:

This narrative is not a justification. Nor should it be read as a confession or a *mea culpa*. What is narrated here is the description of a fact, just as others would describe a sunset or the aroma of a wine. Let me repeat. This narrative is a description of a fact – of the rational actions carried out by a man in full possession of his faculties. The actions of a calm and measured person – an adult if you want. I do not ask for anyone's pity in narrating this. Of course not, since I feel I am not guilty of anything. Lately, a discomfort in the back of my head afflicts me, but I think this is because I sleep very little – not as much as before.

It is true that I have read the Russians and what would that prove with any certainty? That we are influenced by what we read? Such a simple conclusion makes my stomach churn. I will let you know what I read so that you can discard this, from the beginning, as an explanation for the crime. By confessing this I prove that this is not the confession of a lunatic. What is the hypothesis? That the one that narrates all of this is mad. But by narrating this that hypothesis is ruled out. It proves that I am not.

Some people live for others. Some live for themselves – they are selfish. Others live for nothing: they exist, they breathe, they have a place in the world. They even make others believe that there is a purpose, a logic to life with the future unfolding from the present, the present from the past in an orderly way. That there is a logic to each of our daily actions which can be explained and, perhaps, be understood. But is there? (This is a conclusion *a posteriori*. Do not see in these words any connection with the facts of this case.)

We only exist because we breathe. The process is simple: our lungs absorb air through the mouth or nose, and, mechanically we extract oxygen from the air. The heart then pumps this blood, circulating the oxygen through our body. Therefore I exist because I breathe – not because I think – and I will continue to exist as long as I am breathing.

The subway trains came and went as I waited for mine. I thought for a while that it would not be wrong to think that there was a specific subway train for each moment in life. To board any other than mine would result in a missed opportunity.

When the doors opened I saw that there were three people in the car: 3 not 4. THREE. Yes 3, must I repeat it? My heart began racing and I knew immediately and with certainty that one of these three would die before arriving at the next station. I got on and the door closed. I stood with my back to it. Which one of them would die? I had less than a minute to decide.

The first passenger was an old man of 65 or 70. These days it is hard to tell. I saw him as if from a bird's eye view. He had a nervous tic: his right eye blinked as if he were laughing in your face. He was bald and so skinny that you could imagine that he would be dead within two years. If, having asked him, he might say, perhaps: "Choose me, I want to die. What do I care about living another two years more or less! Haven't I lived long enough?" Or perhaps he would express himself otherwise: "No I don't want to die. Two years is two years." And such a selfish thought would wish us to make him a candidate for death – and quickly. But, one way or another, he was not going to die. I knew it with the same certainty that I have in spelling my name backwards.

The second was a young man. He wore his hair in a punk style, red on top, blue on the sides; rings in the ears, eyebrows and chin; black clothes and a broken shoe. Surely he would mock at society, at me watching him, at who knows if not God himself? His fate, one would guess, would be to commit suicide next month or the month after that. (*This paragraph was crossed out but was included in the case by court order.*) We would not be wrong in thinking that he would volunteer to die if we chose him at that time. He was immersed in the music that was reverberating in his ears. It could be heard from where I was standing. It would be a shame to interrupt to tell him that he was not going to die.

The third one was another young man of about 22, or 25 at most. I knew that I was going to kill him the moment I saw him. We looked at each other and in those eyes, which some believe are the mirror of the soul, I could see that he had his whole life ahead of him. He had a rose in his hands, perhaps for his mother or maybe for his girlfriend? He had the face of one who imagines that he will inherit the world of tomorrow. If I were to tell him that he was going to die he would not believe me. "It cannot be," he would tell me. "It is not my time. I refuse." In that one look I learned more about him than from anything that he might have said. In his eyes there was also the loneliness of the modern man, apathetic toward faith, yet desiring to show that he was someone of consequence. For many reasons I chose that he would die. This paltry assertion proves my sanity.

Arriving at the next station, I decided to wait a few seconds so there would be witnesses. The first shot was to his knee so that he would suffer and wish to live a little longer. (Forgive me for the smile on my lips while I narrate this.) The other passengers turned their heads in amazement. The second shot was to his stomach. The other passengers did not know what to do. As the subway train drew to a stop a few people approached the car dumfounded. The third shot hit him in the geometric centre of his skull. (Why make him suffer anymore?) He fell dead like a heavy trunk full of dirty clothes.

I did not try to escape. Nor did I deny what I had

done, nor erase the fingerprints from the gun. No, on the contrary I confessed honestly. When I was arrested, I explained, when asked, how I had killed him. I even told them that it was the punk's right shoe that had a small hole in it; the other shoe was fine. I showed sanity in each of my statements to police. I did not hamper their work. I helped them.

They never asked me why I did it. If they had they would thought that I was mad. But I am not. I have already proved that I am not by narrating these facts logically and rationally.

I have been a model prisoner. And to prove my sanity once more, I have asked for the death penalty.

To the parents of the young man I explained that I had nothing against their son. That I did not kill him for some personal settling of scores or because he was walking down the wrong path. I assumed the reverent posture of he who knows that he has done the right thing. I explained that I had killed him for nothing. Accept my apologies if my narrative, brief up to here, is lacking in details.

Printed in Great Britain
by Amazon